# Henry
## The Hobby

## by BOB GODFREY
## and STAN HAYWARD

HODDER AND STOUGHTON
LONDON SYDNEY AUCKLAND TORONTO

Henry's Cat had just seen a
programme about different hobbies.

One man had the largest collection of bicycle clips in the world.

Then there was a little girl who painted with her feet...

... and a lady who knitted woolly things for horses.

Henry's Cat thought about it more and more.

Douglas Dog liked flying kites.

Sammy Snail did tightrope walking.

Phillipe Frog sang and played the
ukelele.

Ted Tortoise practised boxing...

...and Denise Duck did water-skiing.

All his friends had hobbies.

He met Chris Rabbit, who was busy
looking through binoculars.

It was Chris at <u>his</u> hobby.

Henry's Cat thought this was a <u>very</u> exciting hobby.

He didn't see any flying saucers though.

But he <u>did</u> see a strange man who <u>also</u> had some binoculars…

...and he was looking at a <u>strange</u> bird building its nest.

It went into a hole in the tree to get all the building materials…

...and had soon built a beautiful nest.

The man came out of the bushes and greeted both Henry's Cat and Chris.

He thought they were birdwatchers
like him, so he took them home to tea...

...and Henry's Cat decided that birdwatching was just his sort of hobby.